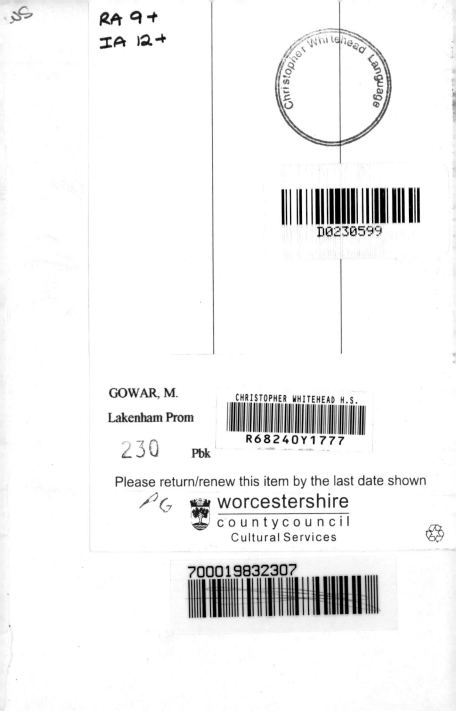

Lakenham Prom

Mick Gowar

Illustrated by Clare Heronneau

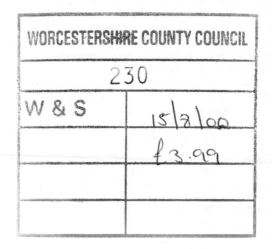
A & C Black • London

GRAFFIX

First paperback edition 2000
First published 2000 in hardback by
A & C Black (Publishers) Ltd
35 Bedford Row, London WC1R 4JH

Text copyright © 2000 Mick Gowar
Illustrations copyright © 2000 Clare Heronneau
Cover illustration copyright © 2000 Mike Adams

The right of Mick Gowar to be identified as author
of this work has been asserted by him in accordance
with the Copyrights, Designs and Patents Act 1988.

ISBN 0-7136-5216-0

A CIP catalogue for this book is available from
the British Library.

Printed and bound in Spain by G. Z. Printek, Bilbao.

Chapter One

8

9

The end

starring
Cindy Lee

As the signature tune for
the News began, Paula
jumped off her bed and
turned the TV off.

Wouldn't it be
wonderful if we could go to
Hollywood High – instead
of grotty old Lakenham
Middle School?

Sally sighed.

All those gorgeous
hunky boys instead of all the
bean-poles and nerds we've
got at Lakenham Middle.

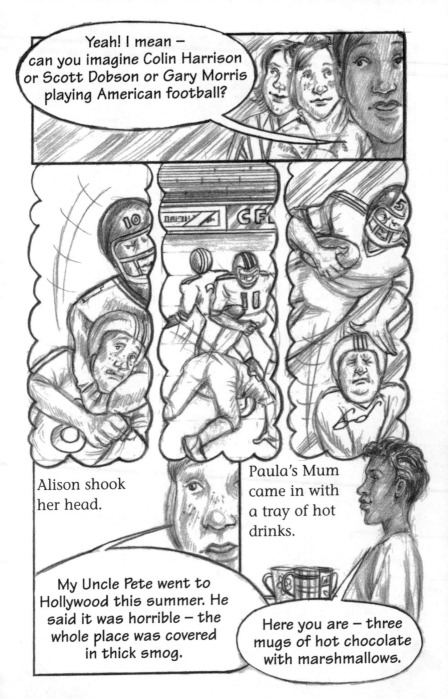

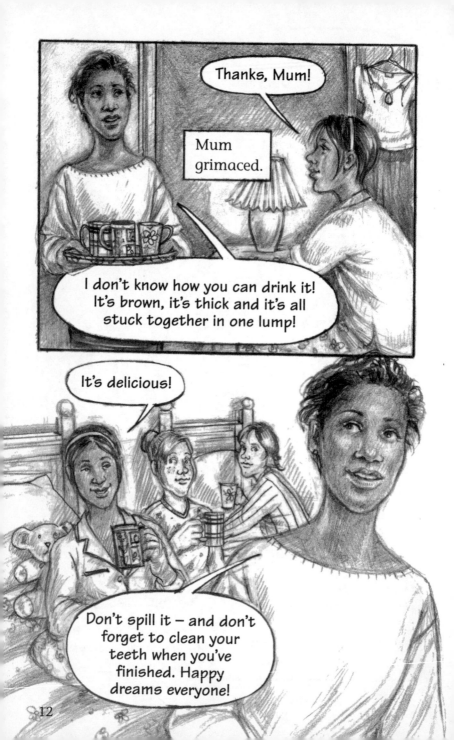

13

Chapter Two

As you know, Christmas is coming and the holidays will soon be here.

There were loud cheers from some of the pupils.

Which means, among other things, end-of-term tests and reports!

There were loud groans from the same pupils.

land of hope
and glory
I know you're keen on music, Alison – but a Prom! The orchestra alone would cost a fortune! No, we couldn't possibly stage our own Prom. That's a very silly idea!

In the staffroom, Mr Tomkins told Miss Kirwin about Alison's idea.

I've just had the most extraordinary suggestion from Alison Coombes.

I asked Class 8 what they'd like to do for a Christmas party this year, and she asked if they could have a Prom!

Miss Kirwin poured herself a cup of tea as if she'd heard nothing out of the ordinary.

Yes...

You don't watch much TV, do you?

You don't seem very surprised. I think it's a bizarre idea! The Last Night Of The Proms at Lakenham Middle School!

And the other girls were all in favour of it, too.

I don't understand. What's that got to do with it?

She didn't mean a Prom like a Promenade Concert at the Albert Hall! She meant an American High School Graduation Dance. Those are called Proms as well. Actually, I think it's quite a good idea – it might be more interesting than the usual boring disco.
Oh, dear! I said it was a daft idea and refused to discuss it.
Call another meeting for lunchtime tomorrow, then I can come along, too. I think you need some help.
And one last thing: watch a show called 'Hollywood High' on TV tonight. You might learn something about American High School Proms!

Chapter Three

That evening, Paula, Alison and Sally watched the latest episode of 'Hollywood High'. It was the big night: Prom Night!

Oh, Chip! I'm so glad we got that silly misunderstanding over Buddy Bolden sorted out.

Me too, Barbie-Sue. If I'd known he'd only been giving you a lift to the Animal Hospital to visit your sick puppy I would never have acted so jealous!

Hollywood
And now, the moment you've all been waiting for: the Prom King and Queen!
Miss Bullwinkle and I have counted your votes for the most popular students, and the winners are... Chip Cracknell and Barbie-Sue Canderell!

Chapter Four

At lunchtime the next day the class met again to discuss the Christmas party.

I'd better start with an apology to Alison, Sally and Paula. I didn't understand what you meant yesterday by a Prom.

Miss Kirwin has explained it all to me. That's why she's here too, to help us with our plans.

Sally, Paula and Alison couldn't believe their ears!

I think a Prom might be a very good idea. So, what sort of things would you like to happen at your Prom?

28

Before Paula could object, Miss Kirwin carried on in a brisk and businesslike way.

Let's have a vote: who would like to have a Prom with a talent competition?

Every hand in the room went up.

That's settled then. But we'll have to start getting things ready right away. It's only two weeks to the end of term!

Several hours later, Paula and Sally were looking at Alison critically.

I'm feeling down, baby –
Really low.
No letter from you –
Not a word.
So I'm sitting here, baby
By my front door –
Waiting for the mailman
To knock on my door.

At the same time, on the other side of the village...

I've got a brilliant idea for how we can win the talent competition.

Scott was a bit doubtful. He'd experienced a number of Gary's good ideas in the past. They usually involved kicking footballs, and they always seemed to end in trouble of some sort.

Oh yeah?

Scott looked even more doubtful.

I suppose we could give it a try. I thought you said Colin was coming.

On the other side of the village, in Paula's bedroom, the dance rehearsal wasn't going too well...

That's the third time you've fallen over. It's really easy! Look – you just do a spin – like this – when they sing *Even a postcard would do*.

He is. I'll go and give him a ring. While I'm doing that, you can be thinking about what we can write a rap about.

Alison picked up her coat and left quickly, so that Paula and Sally wouldn't see how upset she was.

On the other side of the village, Gary was on the phone to Colin.

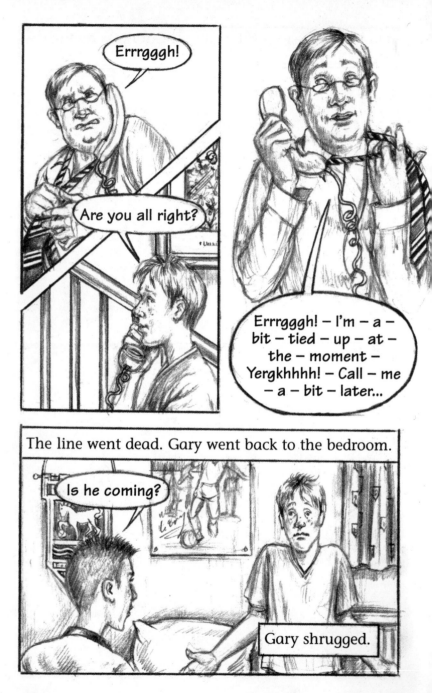

43

There was a
long silence.

45

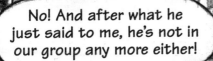

47

Chapter Five

The next week, the countdown to the Lakenham Prom began:

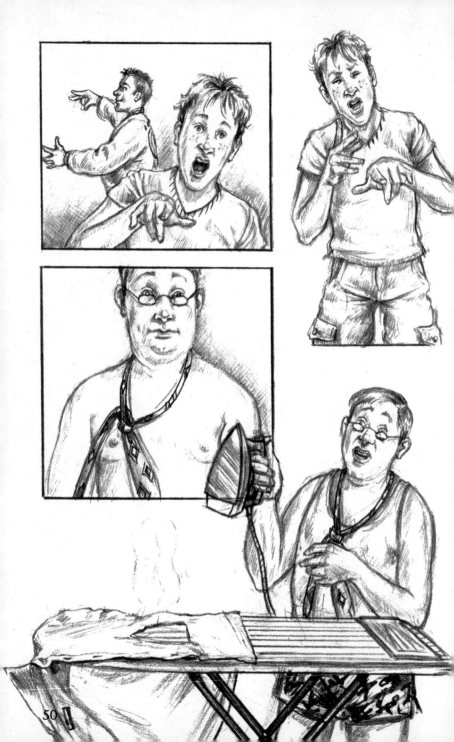

Everything seemed to be going very well, until:

Hello, Alison! The bell's gone. You should be on your way home. What's the matter?

Nothing, Miss. I'm all right.

You don't look all right, Alison. Go on – tell me what's wrong.

Well, Miss, it's the talent competition. I was supposed to be doing a dance with Paula and Sally, but I wasn't any good. And now they won't let me be in it!

Alison gave a deep sigh.

Alison thought for a moment.

Miss Kirwin smiled.

Maths and Art.

No, Alison. We're talking about a talent competition. What do you do outside schooltime?

Well, I play the clarinet, Miss.

Then why don't you play the clarinet at the talent competition?

But, Miss – there's only four days to go! I wouldn't have time to learn a new piece.

53

The picture on my tee-shirt was taken from a genuine x-ray of me! It's exactly what I look like underneath.

Isn't this great, Colin...?

But Colin didn't reply.

Colin...?

But Colin was staring at the screen open-mouthed with his eyes wide.

That's it! That's what I'll do!

What is?

Colin rushed out of the room.

That is! All I need is a black felt-tip and my old white long-sleeved tee-shirt!

What was he talking about?

Chapter Six

At last, the great day – Prom Day!
Paula and Sally were in Paula's
bedroom.

Sally put them on, but she suddenly found walking was very difficult.

They're not very... comfortable, are they? I don't think I could wear them all night.

Don't worry, it'll be fine!

Are you sure this is a good idea?

Of course!

Paula looked up at the clock.

Time to go!

In the lane outside, Paula's dad had just finished cleaning his van.

You two look very nice! Where are you off to?

The School Prom. I told you all about it, don't you remember?

Would you like a lift?

Oh, well – suit yourselves.

Oh, Dad! Not in the van! You're supposed to go to a Prom in a limousine. We'd rather walk.

In the school hall, the Prom was just getting started. Miss Kirwin was trying to encourage the girls to dance.

This is fun, isn't it?

The boys watched while the girls danced. Mr Tomkins tried to persuade the boys to join in.

Come on, boys! Why don't you ask the girls to dance?

...Ipswich...

...Arsenal...

...hooked a big 'un...

Sally and Paula forgot they were in a competition.

And now our next entrants – Gary and Scott with 'The Lakenham Rap'!

Gary and Scott struck appropriate rapper-style poses and began.

Tsh! Pssh! Tsh-tsh! Pssh!

Lakenham is really neat – There's lots of fields of sugar beet!

Tsh! Pssh! Tsh-tsh! Pssh!

The village hall is painted white – There's Youth Club there on Thursday night!

Tsh! Pssh! Tsh-tsh! Pssh!

We're Lakenham boys – we get on down! We watch football at Ipswich Town!

67

When Gary and Scott finished everyone clapped. Several more acts followed. Lee Trotter did a card trick...

And Derek Smalls did his Elvis impersonation.

And your card is – the seven of diamonds!

Very nearly!

And now, for our last act, Alison will play the clarinet.

Alison stood on stage and looked out at the audience.

Go on, Alison! You can do it!

Alison shut her eyes and brought the clarinet to her lips. A plaintive wail soared up the scale, and the melody filled the hall. When she finished there was a moment of silence, and then thunderous applause.

Well done! But I hope you thanked Mr Tomkins and Miss Kirwin for all their hard work in putting on your party.

Go back and say thank you! It'll only take a minute...

But Dad...

Alison didn't say anything.

Go on!

Alison went back into the school. The hall was in darkness, but there was still a light on in the staffroom. As Alison approached the staffroom she heard voices.

Thank you so much for all your help. Without you there wouldn't have been a Prom.

That's very kind. Any time you need help – with anything – just ask me!

She peeped round the door.

Alison decided that perhaps her thanks could wait until Monday. She slipped quietly away, leaving Mr Tomkins and Miss Kirwin alone together.

Chapter Seven